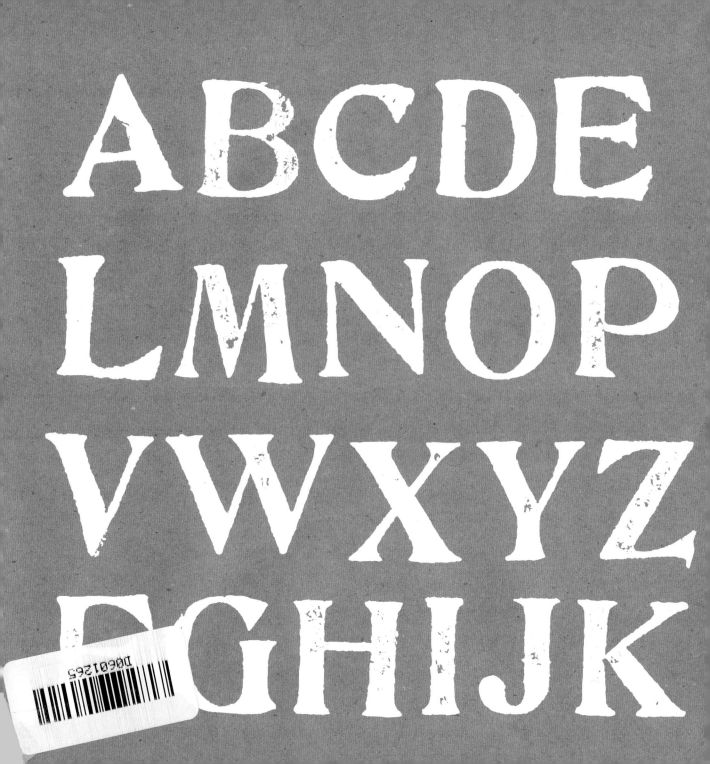

The Land of the Free and the Home of the Brave

Sandra Magsamen is a best-selling and award-winning artist, author and designer whose meaningful and message-driven art has touched millions of lives, one heart at a time. She loves to travel and has had many awesome adventures around the world. For now, she lives happily and artfully in Vermont with her family and their dog, Olive.

A big thank you to my amazing studio team of Hannah Barry and Karen Botti. Their creativity, research tenacity and spirit of adventure have been invaluable as we crafted the ABC adventure series.

Sandra Magsamen

Text and illustrations © 2016 Hanny Girl Productions, Inc. www.sandramagsamen.com
Exclusively represented by Mixed Media Group, Inc. NY, NY.
Cover and internal design © 2016 by Sandra Magsamen

Published by Sourcebooks Jabberwocky, an imprint of Sourcebooks, Inc.
P.O. Box 4410, Naperville, Illinois 60567-4410
(630) 961-3900
Fax: (630) 961-2168
www.sourcebooks.com

Library of Congress Cataloging-in-Publication data is on file with the publisher.

Source of Production: Leo Paper, Heshan City, Guangdong Province, China
Date of Production: November 2015
Run Number: 5004884

Printed and bound in China.
LEO 10 9 8 7 6 5 4 3 2 1

adventure

an end,
can go
A and
again!

Y is for **yummy** eats like apple pie that we love the most.

X is for XOXO

'cause we love to travel the country and see its treasures as we roam.

W is for the **White House,** where the President of the United States makes their home sweet home!

V is for **voting.**

We get to elect the officials we trust.

T is for our **terrific troops** who protect the red, white and blue!

R is for Mt. **Rushmore**

Here, former presidents become "**rock stars**" at this splendid sight!

O

is for our **Olympic** athletes who compete for us with skill, heart and pride.

N is for NASA.

Exploring
solar systems
is the goal!

M is for our marvelous music

like jazz, hip-hop and soul.

L is for the Statue of Liberty. She reminds us that united we stand!

K is for **kayaking** down beautiful rivers and streams all across this great land.

I is for the Declaration of **Independence.** It states

life, liberty and the pursuit of happiness

we are our own nation once and for all.

G
is for our **gorgeous,**

wonderful country that spans from sea to shining sea.

F is for Fourth of July fireworks.

Let's celebrate our freedom and our name!

E

is for the

eagle,

a proud symbol of America and all it overcame.

D

is for **dreaming big.**

Here, you can be your best.

C

is for
cowboys
that roam

the open
land
out West.

B

is for
barbecues

soda

with hot dogs and
sodas that fizz.

A is for **awesome** because that's what America is !

The Land of the Free and the Home of the Brave

America is filled with fantastic and beautiful things to see and do. Just follow the **A, B, C's**, there is an amazing adventure waiting for you!

I love America

an ABC adventure

Sandra Magsamen